The Magic Friendship Snow

Andi Cann

I hope you enjoy reading about Puddles, Jojo, and the friendship snow. Please visit my website https://www.andicann.com. When you register your email address, you will receive a free book and be the first to know about new books, special offers, and free stuff! If you have a chance, Puddles, Jojo and I would appreciate you writing a review on Amazon!

Thank you!

Now, the legal stuff.

Published by MindView Press: Hibou

ISBN-13: 978-0-9980214-3-0   eBook
ISBN-10: 0-9980214-3-1

ISBN-13: 978-0-9980214-4-7   Paperback
ISBN-10: 0-9980214-4-7

To friendship!

One of the best things in life.

Jojo was lonely. She did not have any friends. She looked around. It seemed that everyone already had friends.

Mama duck had her ducklings.

White Kitty had her friends, the dragonflies.

Even the little birds on the tree outside her window
kept warm by snuggling with one another.

Jojo was a little bit sad and very lonely. She did not know how to find a friend or even be a friend. One day she decided to try.

She asked the kite to be her friend. It just smiled
and flew away.

She saw White Kitty and asked, "Will you be my friend, White Kitty?"

White Kitty just looked at her and ran away.

She hugged a tree and asked it to be her friend. It just stood there.

She painted the mountain and asked it to be her friend. It didn't say a word.

Maybe the moon would be her friend. But no, the moon did not accept her friendship invitation.

She felt very, very alone. She still did not know how to make friends.

One day it was snowing. Jojo was making heart shapes on her frosty window when she saw something.

It was a little bit of red in the midst of a lot of snow.

What could it be?

Then, she looked more closely. My goodness! It was a snowman.

She went outside and asked, "Mr. Snowman, will you be my friend?"

To her surprise, the snowman said, "Yes! Hi! My name is Puddles. I was made with friendship snow. I teach children how to be good friends."

She and Puddles started doing everything together.

They talked. They made snow angels. They had great fun.

Sometimes, they got mad at one another.

But, then they would make up! As Puddles had promised, Jojo learned how to be a good friend.

One day, Puddles said to Jojo, "spring is coming, I must go away. Keep this heart to remember that you are a good friend. I will see you next winter."

Jojo cried. "But what will I do without you? You're my best friend, my only friend." Puddles replied, "Jojo, I love you. Others will, too. Believe in yourself! Believe in the magic of friendship snow."

It wasn't snowing anymore, but Jojo missed

Puddles. So, she asked Black Kitty to be her friend.

And Black Kitty said, "Yes!"

One day Jojo and Black Kitty were thinking about Puddles, friendship snow, and the heart that Puddles gave her. She missed him.

Then a little boy peeked over the wall near her house. His name was Ned. Jojo took a deep breath and summoned all of her courage and asked, "Ned, do you want to be my friend?" Ned said, "Yes!"

Jojo and Ned hiked together. They had fun together.

They talked about everything.

Jojo told Ned all about Puddles and the magic of friendship snow.

When summer was over, Ned had to move away.
Sadly, Ned asked Jojo if she thought Puddles would
give him some friendship snow. He wanted to use
the magic to make friends at his new home.

Jojo went to see Puddles. She was sad but wanted to be a good friend to Ned. Jojo took a deep breath and told Puddles about Ned.

Her lips trembled as she asked Puddles, "Ned is nervous about moving to a new home. He won't have any friends. I will miss you. But, will you go with him so that he has a friend?"

Puddles hugged her. "Jojo, you have learned about putting others first. You are kind and generous. You have learned what it means to be a friend. I am going to introduce Ned to my friend, Sunny. Sunny is also made with friendship snow. She will be Ned's friend at his new home."

Jojo missed Ned but knew he was in good hands with Sunny. Jojo made many new friends, too. Every winter Puddles returned, and together they would have fun in the friendship snow.

The End.

Thank you very much for reading 'The Magic of Friendship Snow.' Isn't it a fun story?

If you want a free book and want to learn more about other fun books and characters, please visit my website https://www.andicann.com and register for free materials and special offers.

If you have a chance, Puddles, Jojo, and I would appreciate it if you would write a review on Amazon! Thank you!

Other books by Andi Cann include:

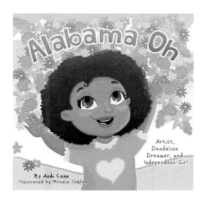
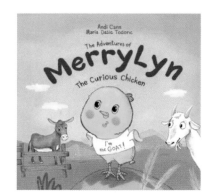

Made in the USA
Monee, IL
16 December 2020